Mama Rex & T

The (Almost) Perfect Mother's Day

by Rachel Vail

illustrations by Steve Björkman

ORCHARD BOOKS

An Imprint of Scholastic Inc.

New York

To Mom, who still asks me for stories and still really listens.
Thanks. Happy Mother's Day.
—RV

For every kid who got in trouble for drawing during class.
—SB

Text copyright © 2002 by Rachel Vail.
Illustrations copyright © 2002 by Steve Björkman.

All rights reserved. Published by Orchard Books, an imprint of Scholastic Inc.
ORCHARD BOOKS and design are registered trademarks
of Watts Publishing Group, Ltd., used under license.
SCHOLASTIC and associated logos are trademarks and/or
registered trademarks of Scholastic Inc.

Library of Congress-in-Publication Data available
ISBN 0-439-40718-4; 0-439-46684-9 (pbk.)

10 9 8 7 6 5 4 3 2 1   03 04 05 06 07

Book design by Elizabeth Parisi

Printed in Singapore 46
First trade printing, May 2003

Contents

 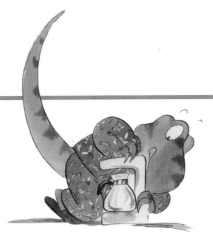

Chapter 1
TIPTOEING

T tiptoed into Mama Rex's bedroom. He wanted to see if she was still sleeping.

It was Mother's Day, and T was planning the perfect surprise present. He was going to make her breakfast in bed.

T couldn't tell if Mama Rex was awake or asleep.

He couldn't see Mama Rex at all. All he saw, in the middle of the bed, was a large lump.

He tiptoed closer, quietly, quietly...

THUMP!

T tripped over a Mama Rex shoe and crashed onto the floor.

"OW!" he said into his hand.

T didn't want to wake up Mama Rex and ruin his surprise of breakfast in bed.

T stood up slowly.
The Mama Rex lump shifted and sighed.
T stood still as a statue, covering his mouth.
The Mama Rex lump stopped moving.
    T watched the floor so he wouldn't trip on any
more shoes. He tiptoed closer, quietly, quietly...

THUMP!

T's tail swatted a pile of magazines on Mama Rex's chair.

T tried to catch the magazines as they fell. Three hit the floor before he got down on his knees. Two plopped into his arms, but then a few slid off his pile onto the others. T dove for those and four more magazines crashed down onto his face.

T raised his arms to protect his head and hit the chair by mistake.

The chair crashed down onto T.

"OW!" T whispered into his hand again.

T lay still under the magazines, the chair, and something silky that had wafted down on top of the whole pile.

He listened for Mama Rex sounds.

T heard a groan and a flop.

He stayed still and counted to fifty-three. He was going to count to 100 but he got a cramp in his hip.

T lifted the chair off himself. A few magazines slid down onto the floor.

T counted to two.

His hip really needed to straighten out. So T stood up quietly, quietly...

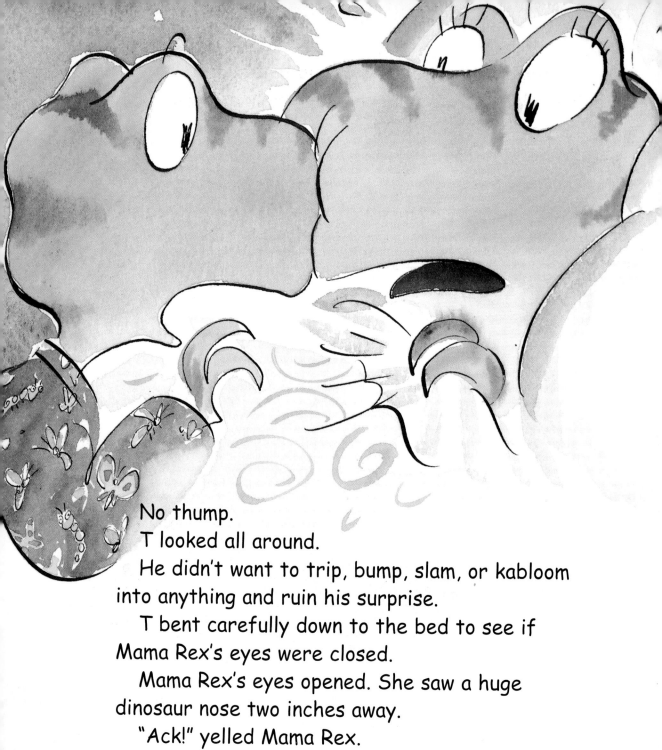

No thump.

T looked all around.

He didn't want to trip, bump, slam, or kabloom into anything and ruin his surprise.

T bent carefully down to the bed to see if Mama Rex's eyes were closed.

Mama Rex's eyes opened. She saw a huge dinosaur nose two inches away.

"Ack!" yelled Mama Rex.

"Yikes!" yelled T.

Mama Rex sat up in bed and gathered
her blankets around her. She was breathing
very fast.

"T!" she gasped. "What are you doing?"

"I wanted to see if you were asleep," explained T.

"I'm not anymore," said Mama Rex.

T frowned. "Could you be?" he asked.

"In a heartbeat," said Mama Rex.

Mama Rex flopped back down and pulled the covers up to her eyebrows.

"Great," whispered T. "On with the plan!"

Chapter 2
A MESS

T ran to the kitchen and flipped on the light.
What Mama Rex liked best for breakfast
was coffee. Coffee in her favorite mug,
which T had made for her. Coffee and also
pancakes. And if Mama Rex loved coffee and
pancakes, that is exactly what T would make for her.

T climbed up onto the counter, beside the coffeemaker.

He tried to remember what Mama Rex did with it to make coffee come out.

T pressed "on."

A red light lit up, but no coffee came out.

T had forgotten to add — the coffee.

T jumped down off the counter and dragged a chair across the room. He stood on the chair and opened the freezer.

A stick of butter dove out and fell on the floor.

T found a bag of coffee, brought it over, and poured some beans into the swing-out part of the coffeemaker, then closed it.

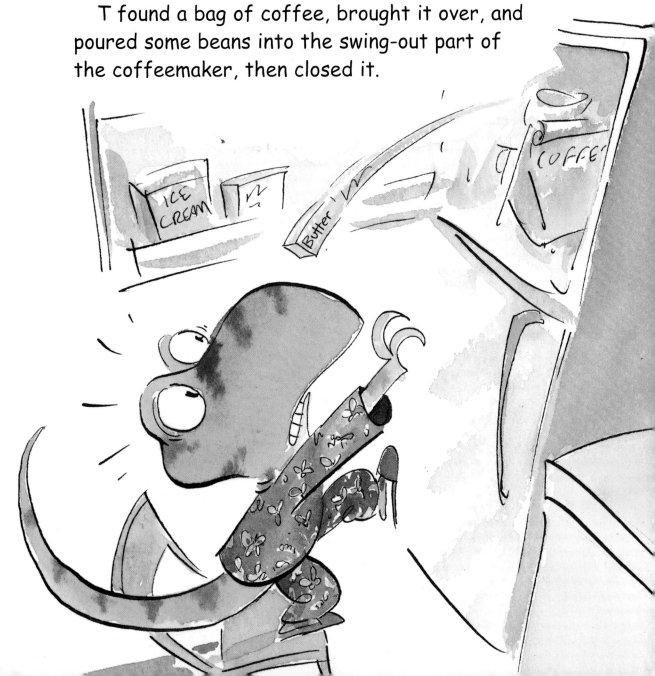

Still nothing.

"Oh, yeah," said T.

T dragged the chair to the sink and filled the pot with water.

Just like Mama Rex, T left a trail of water puddles along the kitchen floor.

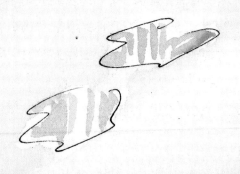

T climbed back up onto the counter and poured the rest of the water in the top of the machine.

Right away it started burping and clucking.

"Hooray," T said to himself. "Now for the pancakes."

T rummaged through the refrigerator and found the box of pancake mix. On the back of the box was a picture of two eggs and a bottle of oil.

"Ingredients," whispered T wisely.

He had made pancakes before, with Mama Rex.

T took two eggs from the carton in the refrigerator and climbed back onto the counter for the oil.

The counter was wet, brown, and hot.

The coffee machine was going crazy, splurting coffee all over the counter. It sounded very proud of itself, burping and splurting and zitsing.

"Stop!" yelled T.

He grabbed the pot and shoved it under the coffee stream.

With the coffee machine more humbly ploomping, T cracked the two eggs into the bowl.

Hardly any shell got in.

He looked at the other ingredients.

Mama Rex always used the little cups with handles for those.

T poured oil into a few cups and pancake mix into the others.

He dumped it all in and stirred, trying to remember what came next.

Ploink. A drop of coffee dripped off the counter onto T's head.

T grabbed a towel off the stove handle and threw it onto the big coffee puddle on the counter and remembered — next comes *cooking* the pancakes.

On the stove.

But T was not allowed to turn on the stove. Ever.

T sat down on the kitchen floor.

Nothing was working.

There was only one dribble of coffee in the pot.

Unless Mama Rex wanted to come lick it off the counter, or suck it from the dish towel, she would have almost no coffee to drink.

And if she wanted to eat pancakes, they would have to be raw.

"This is a terrible Mother's Day," moaned T.

He stood up to glare at the horrible coffee machine and noticed — the toaster oven. He was allowed to toast!

T pulled out the tray and dropped a perfect spoonful of pancake batter on it.

Humming happily, T put the spoon back in for the second pancake.

The first pancake was taking over the whole tray.

The second one joined it and made one big pancake blob.

T tried to separate them with the spoon but it was no use.

He had made pancake soup.

T decided that if Mama Rex liked pancakes, she would *love* toasted pancake soup.

He poured more batter on the tray, shoved it in, and pressed the lever. Then he dragged the chair over to the cabinet to get out Mama Rex's favorite mug and a plate.

T poured the drip of coffee into the mug and went to check the pancake soup.

CLANG! ARR! CLANG! ARR!

The smoke alarm was screaming.

Smoke streamed out of the toaster oven.

T ran toward it and tripped over the mug. One foot slipped on the stick of butter and the other foot splashed down in the bowl of pancake batter.

"Yikes!" T screamed, and floomped into the juicy, battery, buttery lake on the kitchen floor.

Mama Rex ran in.

She opened the toaster oven.

A plume of smoke burst out.

She turned off the toaster oven, unplugged it, grabbed the towel off the counter and used it to pick up the tray, which she dumped in the sink, and opened the window.

Then she lifted T up out of the pancake bowl and carried him to the couch.

Mama Rex held T close until everything was quiet.

Chapter 3
PERFECT

Mama Rex and T walked into the park.

Mama Rex sipped coffee from a cardboard cup with a plastic top. T had milk.

"What a beautiful morning," said Mama Rex.

"Not to me," said T. "To me it's a ruined morning."

Mama Rex sat down on a bench and opened her paper bag. She pulled out a bagel with cream cheese and offered T half.

T shook his head.

"It's Mother's Day," said Mama Rex, taking a bite of her half. "And I know just what I'm hoping for."

"I hope it's not breakfast in bed," said T, kicking a rock.

Mama Rex laughed. "No," she said, leaning back and looking at the sky. "Not breakfast in bed. You end up sleeping in crumbs. Something better."

"I don't have anything, Mama Rex," said T.
He searched on the ground for a perfect round
rock to give Mama Rex.

"Nothing?" asked Mama Rex.

T sadly shook his head. The rocks were all
jaggedy. "Nothing."

T slumped down next to Mama Rex and leaned
his head against her arm.

"Too bad," said Mama Rex. "I was really
hoping for a story. Something funny."

"Nothing's funny to me today," mumbled T.

"How about the young dinosaur who sat on cream cheese?"

"I don't know that one," said T.

"Yes you do," said Mama Rex, pointing at T's tail.

T stood up and peeled the bagel off his bottom. "Oops," he said. "Ew."

Mama Rex helped T with a napkin.

"Nah," she said. "*He sat in cream cheese, it was gross, the end.* Too short. What I'd really love to hear is a big funny real story that happened to you sometime. But if you don't have one..."

T jumped up and down. "How about, what happened the time I tried to make you breakfast in bed? This morning?"

"That," said Mama Rex, "sounds perfect."

"Really?" asked T. "That's all you want for Mother's Day? Me telling you a story?"

"More than anything in the world," said Mama Rex.

"OK," said T. "But I have to warn you, there's a lot of thumping and kablooming and splurting and ploinking."

"Oooh," said Mama Rex. "All my favorites."

"OK. Once upon a time," T began. "Not too long ago and not too far away, there was a slightly clumsy dinosaur who tried to make a perfect Mother's Day...."

"And he succeeded," whispered Mama Rex.

"Shh," said T. "Not yet."

T told Mama Rex the whole story, and she
loved every bit of it.
    Especially the floomping.